Presley the Pug
and the Tranquil Teepee

PRESLEY THE PUG AND THE TRANQUIL TEEPEE

A Story to Help Kids Relax and Self-Regulate

Dr. Karen Treisman

Illustrated by Sarah Peacock

Jessica Kingsley Publishers
London and Philadelphia

First published in Great Britain in 2021 by Jessica Kingsley Publishers
An Hachette Company

This story first featured in *Presley the Pug Relaxation Activity Book*,
published by Jessica Kingsley Publishers in 2019

1

A CIP catalogue record for this title is available from the British Library
and the Library of Congress

ISBN 978 1 83997 031 3
eISBN 978 1 83997 032 0

Printed and bound in Great Britain by Ashford Colour Press

Jessica Kingsley Publishers' policy is to use papers that are natural,
renewable and recyclable products and made from wood grown
in sustainable forests. The logging and manufacturing processes
are expected to conform to the environmental regulations of
the country of origin.

Jessica Kingsley Publishers
Carmelite House
50 Victoria Embankment
London EC4Y 0DZ

www.jkp.com

About this Storybook

Hello, my name is Karen. I am a clinical psychologist, and I am also the author of this fun and creative story about the fantastic, friendly, and helpful Presley the Pug and his canine friends.

This story has helped lots of children around the world to find calm, quiet, peace, relaxation, and some super cool coping tools. You are not alone, and this story is here to help you to:

- understand what makes Presley and his friends feel relaxed, happy, and calm; and what might make them feel worried, stressed, and anxious
- discover a bit more about the magic and helpfulness of creating a special, calm, and safe place in your mind, and in your body
- find some new coping tools and ideas that you can try out if you are feeling unsafe, worried, upset, frustrated, stressed, and much more.

At the end of the story there is a colouring-in page and some questions to help you think a bit more about what you discovered during the story.

If you want even more activities and ideas to support you, have a look at my book *Presley the Pug Relaxation Activity Book*, and card sets *A Therapeutic Treasure Deck of Grounding, Soothing, Coping and Regulating Cards* and *A Therapeutic Treasure Deck of Sentence Completion and Feelings Cards*.

Positive vibes, relaxing thoughts, and floaty feelings!

From Karen, Presley the Pug,
and all of his canine friends

Presley the Pug is a loveable, cheeky puppy. He loves to play, run, sniff, and snuggle up under his cosy soft blanket.

Like all of us, Presley has a rainbow of different feelings inside his head, and inside his body. Sometimes, he feels excited, proud, and happy! Other times he feels angry and frustrated, tired and hungry, sad and lonely, or scared and worried.

Sometimes, we feel a blend of all of these different rainbow feelings — a multi-coloured mix! When feelings become too big, too heavy, or too busy, or if they happen too often, they can feel powerful: very noisy, very bright, and waaay too scary!

Here are some examples of times when Presley's rainbow of feelings became too big.

One time, Presley was having a difficult morning. There had been arguing at home, he had missed the school bus, and he had also forgotten to do his homework.

Another time, Presley had to talk in class about a school project. He felt so nervous and thought everyone would laugh at him and think he was silly. The flutter-flies in Presley's tummy were flapping their wings so hard and fast that he found it hard to think, stay still – or even talk!

Another time, Presley had missed a goal during a game of football. He felt very frustrated and sad, and worried that he had let his team down.

We all feel feelings differently and in our own special way. When Presley feels worried or sad, his thoughts and worries start to spin and whirl. They twist and turn around and around his head until he feels like a whizzing tumble dryer, or as if there's a busy trapped bee frantically buzzing around: bzzzz! bzzzz! bzzzz!

This buzzing and spinning can make it harder for Presley to concentrate. Suddenly, he can't think clearly. He can start to get confused, snappy, and stressed, and even forget things. Sometimes, it even feels hard to breathe with all of the buzzing and whizzing around in his head. Presley didn't enjoy these whirling thoughts and wondered if he was the only one who felt like this.

So, one day, he decided to find out for himself. Presley decided to write a list of things he wanted to ask and things that he could do. At the top of the list was asking some of his dog friends.

First, he bravely approached Dan the Dachshund. He felt a little nervous as Dan was bigger than him and always seemed so chilled, and Presley hadn't really spoken to anyone about this before. Dan was a cheeky and fun Dachshund, but was also known for being super kind. So, he seemed like a good dog to ask first.

'Dan, do you ever get worried, or stressed about things?'

Dan woofed and did a big nod. 'Yes! Of course, we all do, Presley! I have a long list of things. Sometimes, when I have lots of thoughts and feelings, if you could see inside my head it would look like a messy bowl of spaghetti!'

Presley smiled and sighed a breath of relief. He already felt a bit better knowing that he wasn't alone.

Dan the Dachshund whispered, 'You know what though, Presley? I have something that helps me when I'm feeling worried — it is my secret trick... Would you like me to share it with you?'

'Yes, yes, yes please!' Presley eagerly squealed. Dan announced, 'I take something which I call a "brain break". I have a special place in my mind that I can travel to and visit any time I like. It is a bit like a relaxing holiday.

'It is somewhere where I have felt safe, happy, and relaxed. When I go there, it makes me smile and feel warm inside. It is quiet and peaceful, and I know I can go there any time I want if I need a moment to myself.'

'That is so cool — I would love to have a place like that!' Presley barked, admiringly.

Dan the Dachshund grinned. He was very happy that Presley had asked him and that he could help. 'Well, I didn't always have my special place — someone helped me to find it. They asked me to really think about a place where I had felt safe, happy, relaxed, and calm.

'It took a lot of practice, but I can help you to find your place if you would like me to. I bet if we think about it together we will find one that works for you!'

Presley smiled. 'I would really like that, thanks, Dan. So, where is your special place?'

Dan replied, 'It is a beach I visited a few years ago. I feel very lucky — if I close my eyes, and take a deep breath in, I can travel back any time I like, wherever I am. Sometimes I only visit for a few seconds to that beautiful beach. The best bit is that it is like having your very own time machine!

'I can smell the salty fresh air.

'I can see the sun glistening on the water.

'I can hear the tweeting of the birds and the whooshing of the waves of the sea.

'I can feel the sand on my feet and the glowing, warm sun filling me up and moving all the way up and around my body — from my head to my tippy toes.

'I even have a special name to remind me of it. I call it my "Zen Zone". Sometimes, if my family and friends think I might need a brain break, they just say "Zen Zone" to me and it helps me to relax. Even just talking about it now makes me feel more relaxed and happy, Presley.'

'I like the sound of that, but it is hard to think of one for me,' Presley whimpered.

Dan the Dachshund reassured Presley, 'It can take some time. That is okay — there is no rush. Try thinking of different places that you have visited and really liked and that made you feel happy, safe, relaxed, and calm — places that make you smile when you remember them.

'It should be a place where, if you could click your fingers, you would want to travel back to. Then we can choose which is the best. You can also always change it later if you think of another one!

'Why don't we head to the park and we can ask the others? Maybe they will also have some ideas.' Presley nodded.

He was intrigued to see what the others would say!

As they walked to the park, Dan the Dachshund pointed to the rustling of the trees, which sounded like the sigh and whistle of a huge giant. He showed Presley the multi-coloured rocks on the ground, which shimmered as if they were magic pieces of emerald and diamond.

Dan said, 'You see, Presley, there is magic and beauty all around us. You just have to try to notice it, and to keep looking out for it. It is like looking at the world and the things around us with a whole new set of eyes!

Sometimes, I call this a magical treasure hunt, but instead of having to find hidden treasures, the treasures are actually all around us. We just need to really look and use our inner superhero zooming-in vision!'

Presley blinked and looked again.

This time, he started noticing that some of the trees looked like tall grazing giraffes, that the grass felt so soft and bouncy, like a trampoline, and that some of the leaves looked as if they were love hearts floating in the air. Presley gasped, 'Wow, I've walked past this place a million times, and never even noticed any of those beautiful things!'

When Presley and Dan arrived at the park, they were excited to see lots of their doggy friends and barked excitedly. There were dogs of all shapes and sizes! They spent a long time playing, chasing each others' tails, and racing up and down.

Pickle the Maltese — a ball of fluff like a cuddly teddy bear, affectionate, and curious.

Braxton the Bulldog — mischievous and wise, but also fun!

Harlow the Husky — a caring dog with boundless energy, but a terrible memory!

Savina the Saint Bernard puppy — cool as a cucumber with her sunglasses, but also smart and loyal.

Finally, when everyone was tired of running, Presley the Pug asked the other dogs the same question, 'Do you ever get worried, or stressed about things?'

'Well, I used to,' said Savina the Saint Bernard puppy, 'but then Dan the Dachshund taught me his "brain break" trick, and we all use it now. My special place is floating high in the sky in a hot air balloon.' Savina smiled.

'I went in a hot air balloon on my last birthday, and I felt the happiest and the most peaceful I had ever felt! High in the sky among the fluffy clouds, I felt like a soaring bird gliding through the air!'

Savina carried on explaining, 'I can get worried and jittery when things are too loud or too busy. When there's too much noise at home, or when there are big crowds at school in the classroom, or in the playground, I now know I can take a moment to travel back to that hot air balloon!

'To get there, I imagine I am back in that beautiful hot air balloon, floating around. Then I breathe deeply and imagine the flutter-flies in my tummy flying and flurrying far, far away from me.

'I try to really feel the breezy blue air and the fluffy clouds calmly...slowly...gently...floating through my body and my head.

'Using my imagination helps me to travel back to my relaxing place. I don't like closing my eyes, but I can still visit my balloon with my eyes open.

'What about the rest of you?' Savina asked, looking around at the others curiously.

Harlow the Husky ruffed, 'Well, I really struggle to concentrate, and...oh, what's that over there? A stick?

'Sorry, what was I saying? Oh, yes, I struggle to concentrate...Well, I don't like heights, so no hot air balloon for me, mine is much closer to the ground!

'I actually imagine this park where we are right now – I think about lying under my special wooden bench, looking out at the trees, eating one of my yummy dog biscuits, and smelling my favourite flowers.

'Like Dan, I have a reminder name too. I call it my "Peaceful Park". I'm lucky because I can visit this park in real life, but when I have to stay at home or when it's too cold and rainy, I can still visit it in my mind.'

Harlow woofed, 'Because I find it hard to concentrate, this can sometimes make it difficult for me to travel here in my mind. To help me, Braxton the Bulldog taught me another cool trick. Oh, I love tricks! – I love to jump up on two legs and leap up to catch sticks in mid-air! Hang on, where was I? Come on, concentrate, Harlow...

'Oh yes! Braxton told me a special way of travelling there: to imagine a journey which involves a bit more time to get there. It could be anything – flying in a helicopter, opening a magic door, whooshing down a slide, scampering down some stairs...

'I chose a secret gold and green fairy gate, covered in flowers. So, when I need some help to travel to my Peaceful Park, I picture in my mind the beautiful fairy gate. I imagine opening the magic door, and...slowly...entering the Peaceful Park...

'Sometimes I still struggle, so Braxton has helped me to make my very own fairy gate using wood, paint, stickers, lollipop sticks, and glitter. When I'm finding it really difficult to concentrate, I look at my gate creation, and it helps me to go on my journey to my Peaceful Park.'

Pickle the fluffy Maltese spoke up, 'I have a place like this too! I use it when I am finding it hard to go to sleep, or when I need to do something new which can feel scary, like when I started a new school.

'Mine is a bit different though. I tried for a while, but I couldn't think of an actual place, which made me feel a bit sad, but then Dan the Dachshund told me that I could make up my own imaginary place. So, I did! I call it "Gorgeous Galaxy", and it's amazing!

'I get to travel there on a gold and purple spaceship. I whizz through all the colourful galaxies and then, once I arrive, I chill out on the cool, quiet, glowing moon, surrounded by millions of distant twinkling stars.

Because it is not a real place and it only exists in my mind, it can be a little bit harder to remember the details, especially when I am feeling worried. So, like Harlow's fairy gate, I use objects to help me to remember my special place. I made a poster, a keyring, and a mini model of my Gorgeous Galaxy!'

Presley said, 'Wow, I like this idea. I can't believe you all have one. I bet it would have helped me before my test at school, or when I had an argument with Chilli the Chihuahua yesterday.'

Presley clapped. 'You have all really helped me. I think I have now thought of my own special place! It might change, but let's try it out. I once stayed in a wood surrounded by trees, flowers, and lavender. It felt as if it was enchanted, and I was cuddled up in my very own teepee. I slept under the stars, with all the sounds of nature around me, and mmm, the smell of lavender. There were so many incredible trees. Some of them were twisted and bent so that you could sit inside them and feel as if the tree was actually giving you a huge hug!

'I felt so happy, it was as if I was smiling inside.' Presley's face lit up talking about it, and his shoulders started to relax.

'That is perfect, well done,' said Dan the Dachshund. 'Can you think of a word that will help you to remember that place?' Presley thought for a moment. 'Ummmm, how about Tranquil Teepee?'

'Wow! That is a good name,' barked Savina the Saint Bernard puppy. 'Now see if you can travel back there in your mind. You can close your eyes if you want to. You might like to choose how to travel back there, like Pickle did on her spaceship, or Harlow did through her magic fairy gate.'

Presley yapped, 'Ooh yes, I would like to travel there on the back of my very own colourful pet unicorn.'

'Now that is a great way to travel there!' everyone cheered.

Harlow the Husky croaked, 'Okay, I'm going to help you to go on your journey.

'Imagine you are on your pet unicorn travelling back to your Tranquil Teepee.

'Think about all the things that you can see, smell, feel, hear, and taste when you are there.

'All of our senses can give us great memories and clues. We just need to learn how to use them. This might help too, Presley.' Harlow sprinkled some lavender spray on Presley's star bandana.

Presley took a deep breath in. The lavender smell helped him to travel back to that special place even faster. 'Yes, I can think of all of those things you said.'

Harlow the Husky continued guiding Presley, 'Now take your time. Breathe in your Tranquil Teepee place. Look around you at all the things that you said you could see, hear, feel, smell, and taste while you were there. Notice how your mind and body feel when in your calm, relaxed, and happy place.

'Soak it all in, slow everything down, spend a little time there. When you are ready you can come back to this park, but try to remember and to hold on to those magical, positive, and warm feelings of your Tranquil Teepee place.'

'I enjoyed that, and it actually worked. Next time, I might take my cosy snuggly blanket with me!' Presley cheered.

'I'm so happy I now have my Tranquil Teepee. To help me remember, I'm going to put a picture of it on the front page of my school diary, and a photo of it in my pencil case.'

Braxton the Bulldog suggested, 'To help you at night, you could even make a teepee cover to go over your bed, and we could decorate your pillows with photos and pictures of your Tranquil Teepee place.' 'Ooh, yes, let's do that!' Presley jumped with joy.

Dan the Dachshund added, 'Presley, the secret to making your journey is to practise: the more you practise, the easier it will be to travel there.

'If you can, try and visit your Tranquil Teepee place for a short time every day. We can remind you if you need help. It is like taking your brain for an excercise and will help your brain and body to remember it – we call this "muscle memory" and it is super cool.

'So, when you are feeling upset, stressed, or worried and need a brain break or a magic moment, it will be much easier to get to your Tranquil Teepee. Your brain will have had lots of practice.

'Remember, this is just one trick and there are loads more tricks out there to help. You have lots of choices — you just need to choose some that suit you.'

Dan the Dachshund woofed and moved his body around as if he was made of wiggly jiggly jelly. 'I love moving around — for me, exercise, stretching, and moving around are great ways to release and shake-out the feelings!'

Braxton the Bulldog chimed in, 'Eek, I can't move like that, but I have my own cool tricks. I like to draw, paint, colour, act out, or write down my feelings in my special diary.'

Savina the Saint Bernard puppy nodded, and said, 'I have my own soothing happy box where I keep lots of things which help me feel calm – things I can see, touch, smell, taste, and listen to. Like a stress ball, some happy photos, a glitter jar, a wind chime, a shell, some silky material, and some lavender hand cream.

'My box really helps me to feel much more relaxed and it gives me something to focus on. The best bit is that I can keep on adding to it and doing fun art projects to add to it.'

'Ooh, that looks fun and cool! I want one of those,' yelped Harlow.

Pickle the fluffy Maltese chuckled, 'You can also have more than one place, or a different type of place. I love my Gorgeous Galaxy, and it really helps to make me feel calm and sparkly, but I also have a funny and fun place which I can use the time machine in my mind to visit. It really makes me smile and belly laugh so much and so loudly. This works really well too, and usually turns my frown upside down.'

Harlow the Husky nodded and said, 'I also do lots of breathing and relaxation exercises. My favourite one is called hand or star breathing.' 'What's that?' Presley said, looking puzzled. 'Well, you hold out your hand and you trace your fingers. Then as you trace your fingers, you take a deep breath in as you travel up the fingers, and then a deep breath out when you travel down the fingers. You can even do this before, during, or after you are in your Tranquil Teepee, Presley.'

Presley excitedly barked, 'Wow, thanks so much for your help, everyone. I feel much better now, and have loads of new ideas to try.' Pickle replied, 'Our pleasure, Presley, and this is just the start. You can try these ones out and then let us know what you think, and we can share with you some more special tricks next week!'

Presley now felt as if he had a whole treasure box of tricks, and that he was ready to practise. He could be like a scientist and try them out when he needed a brain break, or just a moment of calm.

A few weeks later, after lots of practising, Presley was feeling a bit worried and stressed, so Harlow the Husky gently looked over to him and calmly whispered, 'Tranquil Teepee'. Presley smiled, sniffed his bandana, took a deep slow breath in, and off he went in his mind on his magical, colourful, unicorn journey to his Tranquil Teepee where there were trees waiting to hug him, the wind waiting to whistle around him, and the sun waiting to fill him up with calm, warm, feel-good vibes.

Have a think about these questions and talk about them with an adult. You can just pick one or two if you like – there is no rush, so take your time. Remember, there are no right or wrong answers.

1. Who is your favourite character from the story, and why?

2. Presley is a fawn pug. If you were a dog or another animal, what would you like to be? What animals would your friends and family be?

3. What was your favourite part of the story, and why? What was your worst part?

4. What things do you think make Presley feel scared, worried, upset, and sad? Are these similar to or different from the things that can make you feel scared, worried, upset, and sad?

5. Presley describes how his worries spin, turn, and twist around in his head like a whizzing tumble dryer, or like a busy trapped bee frantically buzzing around. How do the worries you have make you feel? What words can you use to describe them?

6. What makes Presley feel happier, safer, calmer, and more relaxed? Are these similar to the things that can make you feel happier, safer, calmer, and more relaxed?

7. Lots of different words are used in the story to describe a feeling, such as relaxed, calm, and peaceful. Which word would you use to describe a feeling? What does this look like, feel like, and mean to you?

8. Try to remember the tricks and tools that Presley learns to calm down and to feel happier. What calm-down tricks do you use, or have you seen other people use?

9. Presley's special place is called his Tranquil Teepee and Harlow the Husky's is called her Peaceful Park. Where might your peaceful, happy, calming, and safe place be? What would you name your special place? What does it look like and feel like?

10. Harlow the Husky travels to her Peaceful Park through a gold, green, and flower-filled gate with a magic door. To help her remember this she makes a fairy gate using wood, paint, stickers, and glitter. How would you like to travel to your special place? What could you do or make to remember your journey and your special place?

11. What different senses can Presley use to make his special place feel even more real? What different smells, sounds, sights, tastes, or things to touch make you feel calm?

12. What other adventures do you think Presley and his friends might go on? If you want to, you could write a follow-up story.

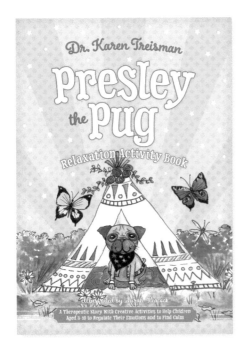

Presley the Pug Relaxation Activity Book

A Therapeutic Story with Creative Activities to Help Children Aged 5–10 to Regulate Their Emotions and to Find Calm

Dr. Karen Treisman

£22.99 | $29.95 | 152PP | PAPERBACK | ISBN: 978 1 78592 553 5 | EISBN: 978 1 78775 110 1

Enjoyed Presley the Pug and the Tranquil Teepee? Try the Presley the Pug Activity Book!

Dr. Karen Treisman has also created a Presley the Pug Activity Book, which features the story you have just read along with a wealth of creative activities about Presley and his friends, all designed to help children to explore feelings. The activity book features reliable advice for adults on how you can help any child who struggles to regulate their emotions and find calm.

Like all dogs, Presley the Pug loves to play, run, and snuggle up under his warm blanket. But sometimes, Presley gets so excited that his feelings take over.

Sometimes it's anger, sometimes stress, sometimes worry. He doesn't know how to calm down! What can Presley do when he feels like this? Luckily Presley's canine friends are nearby with some wise words and they share some of the tricks that have worked for them!

This therapeutic activity book was developed by expert child psychologist Dr. Karen Treisman. It features a colourful therapeutic story designed to help start conversations about coping with big feelings and how to find calm. It explains how Presley (and the reader!) is able to create a 'mind retreat' – an imaginary safe space where he can relax.

The activity book is also packed with creative activities and photocopiable worksheets to help children to explore the ideas raised in the story, including regulating and coping tools like sensory boxes, relaxation exercises and easy yoga poses. It also features advice and practical strategies for parents, carers and professionals supporting children aged 5–10.

Dr. Treisman's Big Feelings Stories

Cleo the Crocodile's
New Home
ISBN 978 1 83997 027 6
EISBN 978 1 83997 028 3

Gilly the Giraffe Learns
to Love Herself
ISBN 978 1 83997 029 0
EISBN 978 1 83997 030 6

Neon the Ninja Meets
the Nightmares
ISBN 978 183997 019 1
EISBN 978 183997 020 7

Ollie the Octopus and
the Memory Treasures
ISBN 978 1 83997 023 8
EISBN 978 1 83997 024 5

Binnie the Baboon
and the Big Worries
ISBN 978 1 83997 025 2
EISBN 978 1 83997 026 9